CHRISTMAS IN THE BARN

CHRISTMAS
in the Barn

BY MARGARET WISE BROWN

ILLUSTRATED BY ANNA DEWDNEY

HARPER

An Imprint of HarperCollinsPublishers

In a big warm barn in an ancient field

The oxen lowed, the donkey squealed,
The horses stomped, the cattle sighed,

And quietly the daylight died
In the sunset of the west.

And a star rose brighter than all stars in the sky.

The field mice scampered in the hay

And two people who had lost their way
Walked into the barn at the end of the day

And they were allowed to sleep in the hay
"Because there was no room in the inn."

The little mice rustled in the sweet dry grass
Near the lambs and the kine and the ox and the ass.

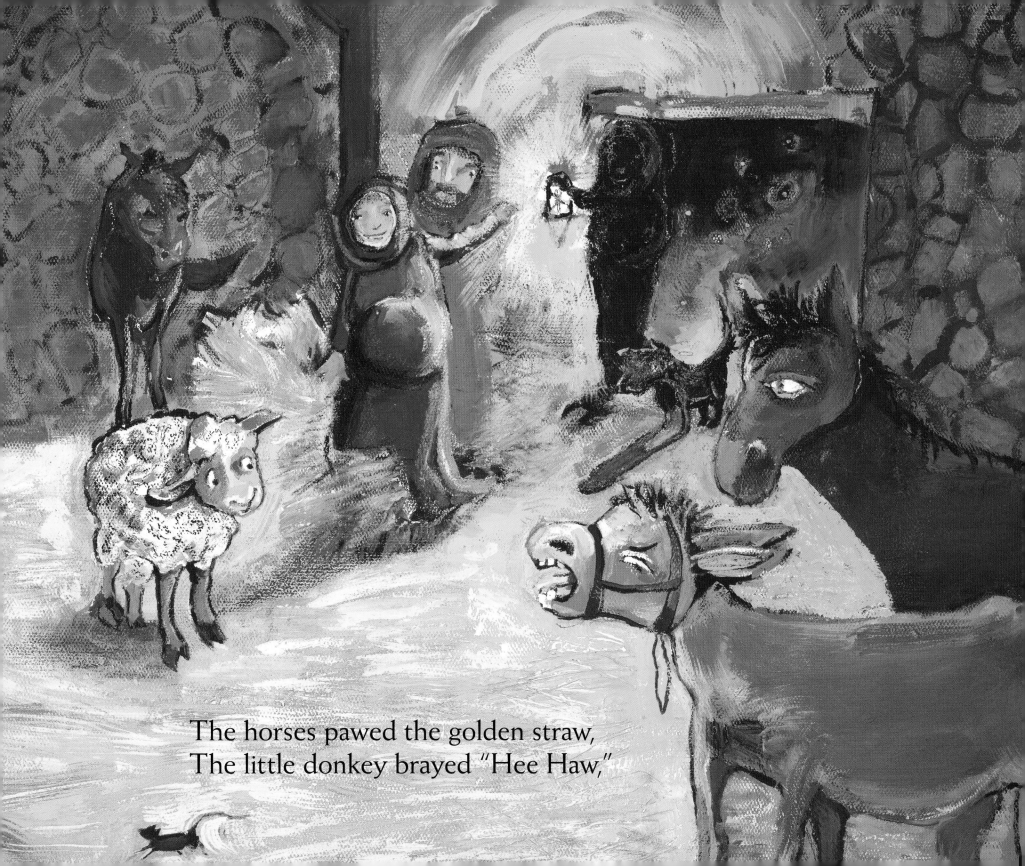

The horses pawed the golden straw,
The little donkey brayed "Hee Haw,"

And there they were all safe and warm
All together in that ancient barn

When hail—the first wail of a newborn babe reached the night
Where one great star was burning bright

And shepherds with their sheep
Are come to watch him sleep.

What child is this who is born here
Where the oxen stomp and peer,

Away in a manger, no crib for his bed
What child is this who lays down his sweet head?

In the big warm barn in the ancient field
The little child sleeps, the donkey squeals

The star goes down
Yet the wise men stay to see the dawning Christmas Day.

The child was sleeping in the hay

And there they were
All safe and warm

All together
In that ancient barn.

Library of Congress Cataloging-in-Publication Data

Names: Brown, Margaret Wise, 1910–1952, author. | Dewdney, Anna, illustrator.
Title: Christmas in the barn / by Margaret Wise Brown ; illustrated by Anna Dewdney.
Description: Newly illustrated edition. | New York : HarperCollins, 2016. | Summary: Rhyming text relating the birth of a
    child in a barn among farm animals.
Identifiers: LCCN 2016000190 | ISBN 9780062379863 (hardback)
Subjects: | CYAC: Christmas—Fiction. | Domestic animals—Fiction. | Stories in rhyme. | BISAC: JUVENILE FICTION /
    Holidays & Celebrations / Christmas & Advent. | JUVENILE FICTION / Animals / Farm Animals. | JUVENILE
    FICTION / Religious / Christian / General.
Classification: LCC PZ8.3.B815 Co 2016 | DDC [E]—dc23 LC record available at http://lccn.loc.gov/2016000190

The artist used oil paint, pastel, pencil, and marker to create the illustrations for this book.
16 17 18 19 20 WOR 10 9 8 7 6 5 4 3 2

Originally published in 1952 by Thomas Y. Crowell Company
First HarperCollins Publishers edition, 2004
Newly illustrated edition, 2016